THE
SQUISHINESS
OF
THINGS

MARC
KOMPANEYETS

ALFRED A. KNOPF
NEW YORK

To my mother, Katya,
and my sisters, Yelena and Tanya

THIS IS A BORZOI BOOK PUBLISHED BY ALFRED A. KNOPF

Copyright © 2005 by Marc Kompaneyets

All rights reserved under International and Pan-American Copyright
Conventions. Published in the United States by Alfred A. Knopf, an imprint of
Random House Children's Books, a division of Random House, Inc., New York,
and simultaneously in Canada by Random House of Canada Limited, Toronto.
Distributed by Random House, Inc., New York.

KNOPF, BORZOI BOOKS, and the colophon are registered
trademarks of Random House, Inc.

Library of Congress Cataloging-in-Publication Data
Kompaneyets, Marc.
The squishiness of things / by Marc Kompaneyets. — 1st ed.
p. cm.
SUMMARY: The great scholar Hieronymus believes
that he knows everything there is to know,
until a hair which he cannot identify is carried
to him on the wind and he must search the globe
to find its source.
ISBN 0-375-82750-1 (trade)
ISBN 0-375-92750-6 (lib. bdg.)
[1. Learning and scholarship—Fiction.
2. Voyages and travels—Fiction. 3. Hair—Fiction.
4. Allegories.] I. Title.
PZ7.K83495Sq 2005 [Fic]—dc22 2004020360

www.randomhouse.com/kids

MANUFACTURED IN MALAYSIA
June 2005
10 9 8 7 6 5 4 3 2 1
First Edition

n a month much like this month and in a year much like this year, Hieronymus stepped on a bug. It was an ordinary bug, not particularly squishy or crunchy, but somewhere in between.

Imagine for a second that you have just stepped on a bug. What would you do? You would do nothing. But Hieronymus did something, and that's why he's world-renowned while you're sitting at home with your nose in this book, reading about his exploits.

Hieronymus immediately saw the need to create a method to measure the crunchy-squishiness of bugs. Did he stop there, as an ordinary genius might? No, for he was no ordinary genius. He then stepped on 16,567 different types of bugs, going through many pairs of shoes, in order to discover the crunchy-squishiness of each bug.

Hieronymus was so wise that he gathered in his head much of what was possible to know under the sun. Of the saltiness of ink he was learned, of the bounciness of sausage he was an authority. He measured the number of lentils it would take to dam up the Nile and studied whether porcupines liked sweet potatoes or yams.

But eventually Hieronymus could not find anything new to measure. For everything that could be measured had been measured, and everything worth knowing became known. There was nothing left to do.

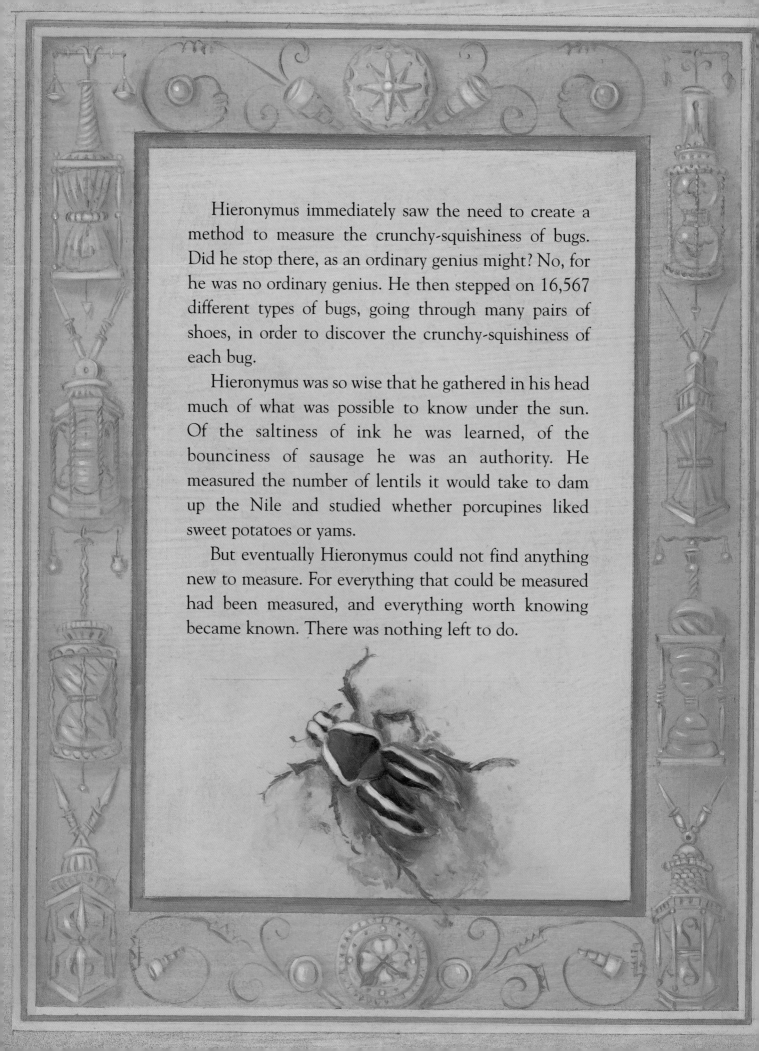

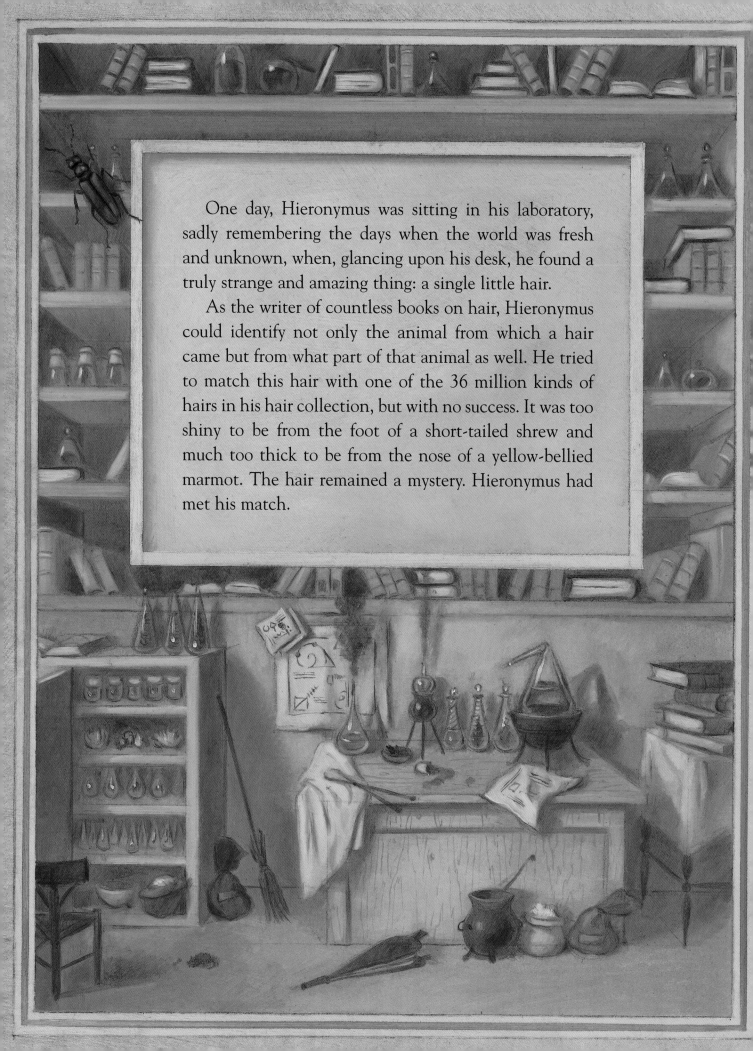

One day, Hieronymus was sitting in his laboratory, sadly remembering the days when the world was fresh and unknown, when, glancing upon his desk, he found a truly strange and amazing thing: a single little hair.

As the writer of countless books on hair, Hieronymus could identify not only the animal from which a hair came but from what part of that animal as well. He tried to match this hair with one of the 36 million kinds of hairs in his hair collection, but with no success. It was too shiny to be from the foot of a short-tailed shrew and much too thick to be from the nose of a yellow-bellied marmot. The hair remained a mystery. Hieronymus had met his match.

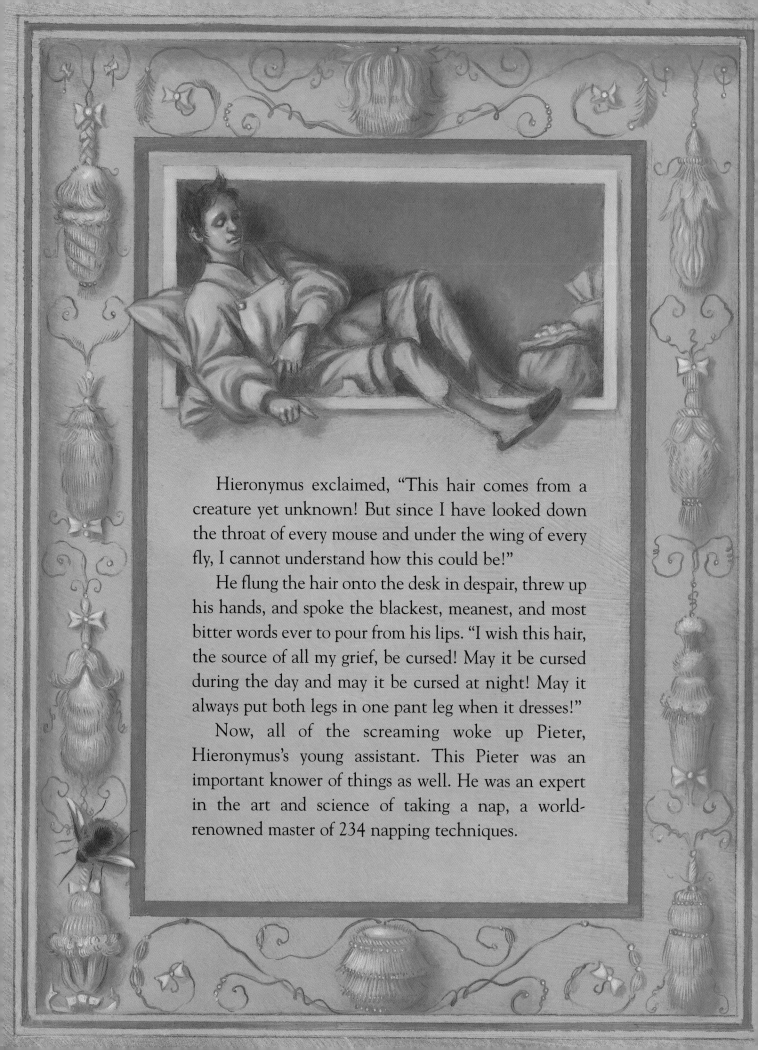

Hieronymus exclaimed, "This hair comes from a creature yet unknown! But since I have looked down the throat of every mouse and under the wing of every fly, I cannot understand how this could be!"

He flung the hair onto the desk in despair, threw up his hands, and spoke the blackest, meanest, and most bitter words ever to pour from his lips. "I wish this hair, the source of all my grief, be cursed! May it be cursed during the day and may it be cursed at night! May it always put both legs in one pant leg when it dresses!"

Now, all of the screaming woke up Pieter, Hieronymus's young assistant. This Pieter was an important knower of things as well. He was an expert in the art and science of taking a nap, a world-renowned master of 234 napping techniques.

Pieter opened only one eye, for he was skilled in the method of being half-asleep and half-awake. "Master," he said, "how can I hope to ever improve my naptitude if you raise a hubbub over every hair the restless winds blow through the window?"

Just then, a gentle breeze blew in from an open window, carrying another hair exactly like the one that came before it.

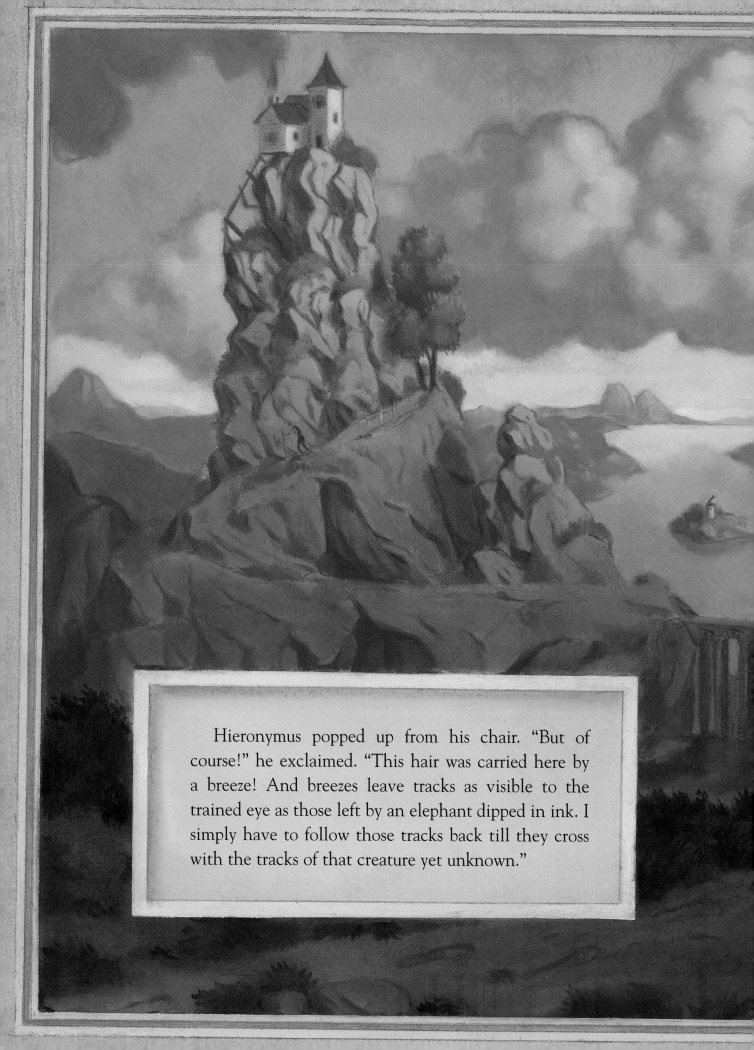

Hieronymus popped up from his chair. "But of course!" he exclaimed. "This hair was carried here by a breeze! And breezes leave tracks as visible to the trained eye as those left by an elephant dipped in ink. I simply have to follow those tracks back till they cross with the tracks of that creature yet unknown."

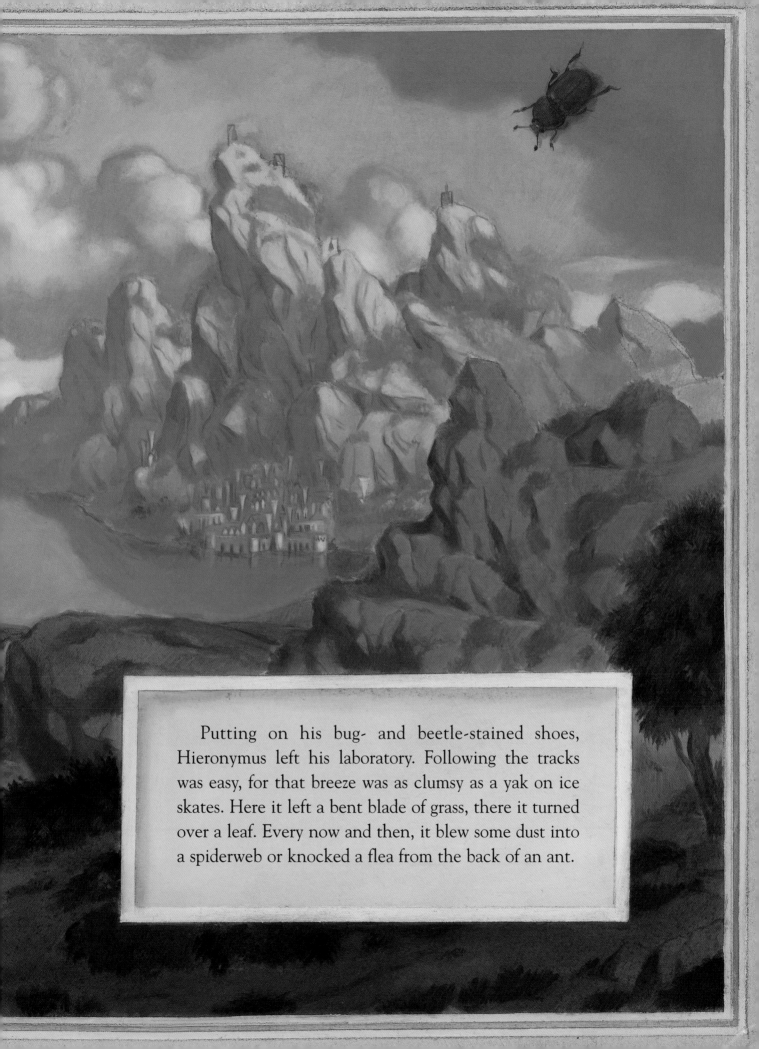

Putting on his bug- and beetle-stained shoes, Hieronymus left his laboratory. Following the tracks was easy, for that breeze was as clumsy as a yak on ice skates. Here it left a bent blade of grass, there it turned over a leaf. Every now and then, it blew some dust into a spiderweb or knocked a flea from the back of an ant.

After walking for many days, Hieronymus entered the strange land of the Bobnatabobs, where the people have a passion for loud noises of all kinds. They enjoy wearing large drums on their heads, which they bang at all hours of the day and night. Their king is always accompanied by noisemakers, selected for their talent for raising a frightful racket.

Hieronymus decided to ask the wisest Bobnatabobs about his hair. But when he tried to speak, they scowled at him and screamed, "Who are you with such a feeble voice to disturb this council of those most wise? For to be wise, one must be loud—and we're the loudest in the land!"

"I seek the source of this," replied Hieronymus, holding up the hair. "For once I know the nature of this thing unknown, I will know all there is to know."

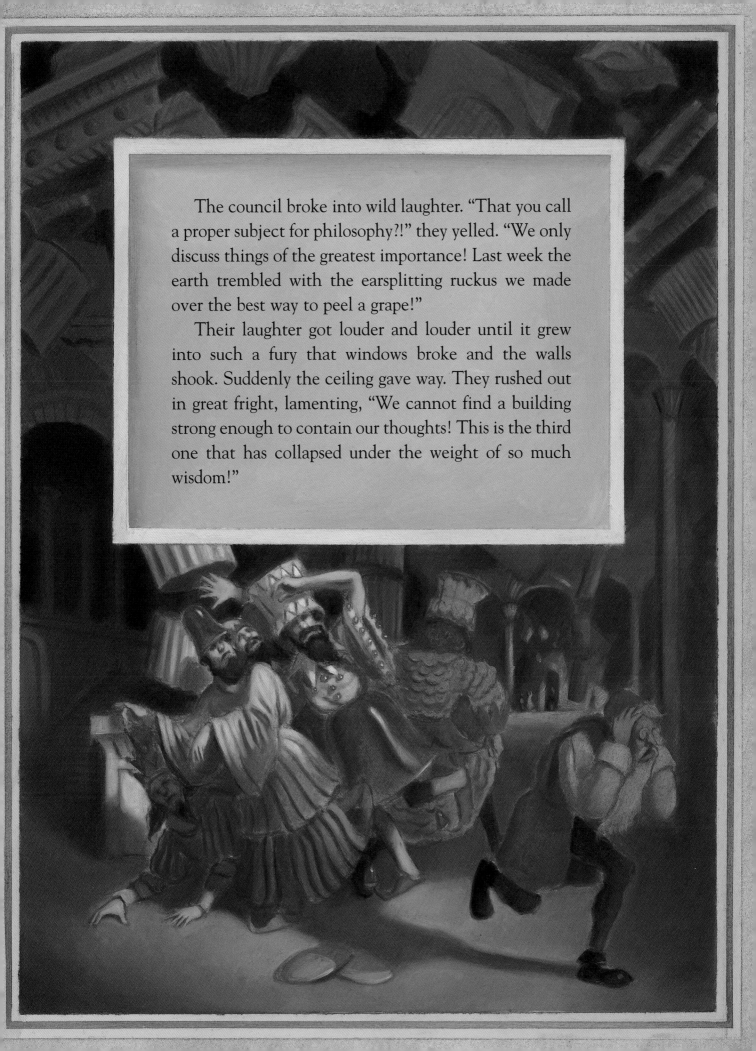

The council broke into wild laughter. "That you call a proper subject for philosophy?!" they yelled. "We only discuss things of the greatest importance! Last week the earth trembled with the earsplitting ruckus we made over the best way to peel a grape!"

Their laughter got louder and louder until it grew into such a fury that windows broke and the walls shook. Suddenly the ceiling gave way. They rushed out in great fright, lamenting, "We cannot find a building strong enough to contain our thoughts! This is the third one that has collapsed under the weight of so much wisdom!"

After another journey of many days through forsaken wilds, Hieronymus entered the kingdom of Pabnayabishland. In this land live the Pabnayabish, who have no memory of things past and think that everything is new under the sun. Each day a thousand geniuses discover laughter, sneezing, and blinking. They go through their lives in sheer delight, experiencing each thing anew.

As Hieronymus passed through this land, he came upon a group of young Pabnayabish singing and dancing in the fields. He approached them and said, "I wish to see the wisest of your land so as to ask them a question of the highest importance."

"Then you have come to the right people, for we are by far the wisest people we know," one of the Pabnayabish replied. "I, for example, have made great contributions to science by discovering that not everything green is edible. The creative genius to my right developed spitting, and the one to my left discovered a way to say things that are not true in a way that makes it seem that they are."

"Then help me, wise people. I have traveled many days and nights in order to find the source of this," said Hieronymus, holding up the hair. "For once I know the nature of this thing unknown, I will know all there is to know."

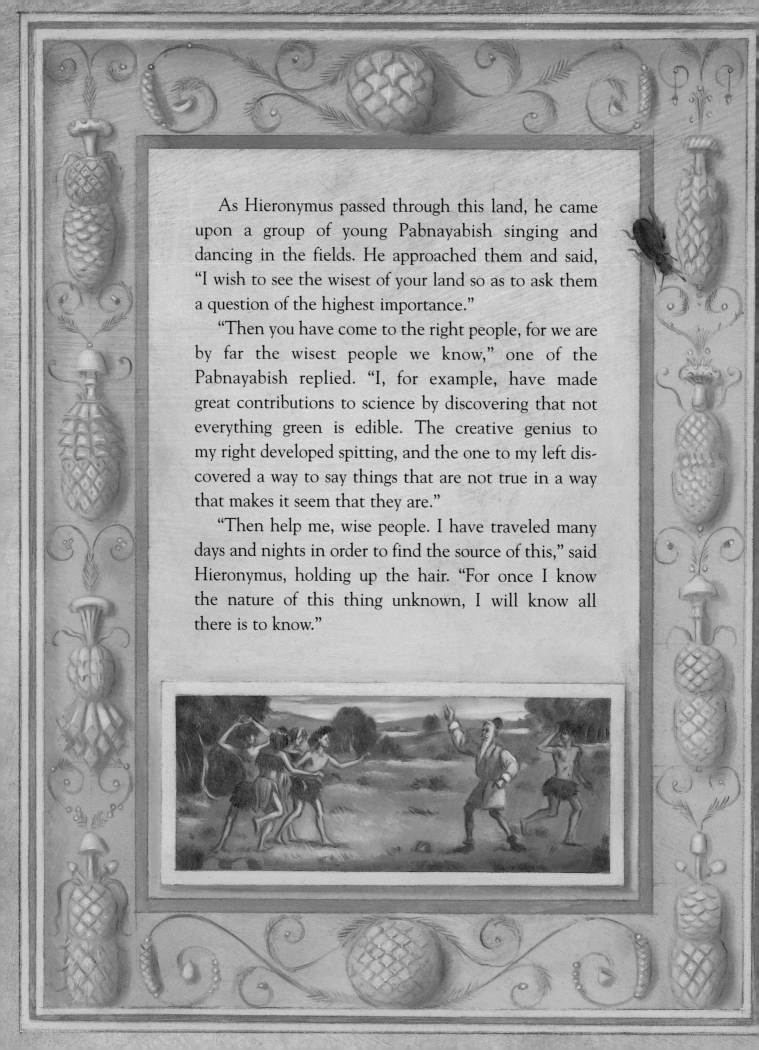

"It seems to me," one of the Pabnayabish said angrily, "that you have stolen my method of speaking in a way that is not true. For no one can travel many days and nights when all of us here know that the world was created yesterday!"

"Aha!!" cried another. "I have discovered that there are people in the world who think we're fools!" They chased after him, until they forgot what they were so angry about and resumed their dancing and singing as if nothing had happened.

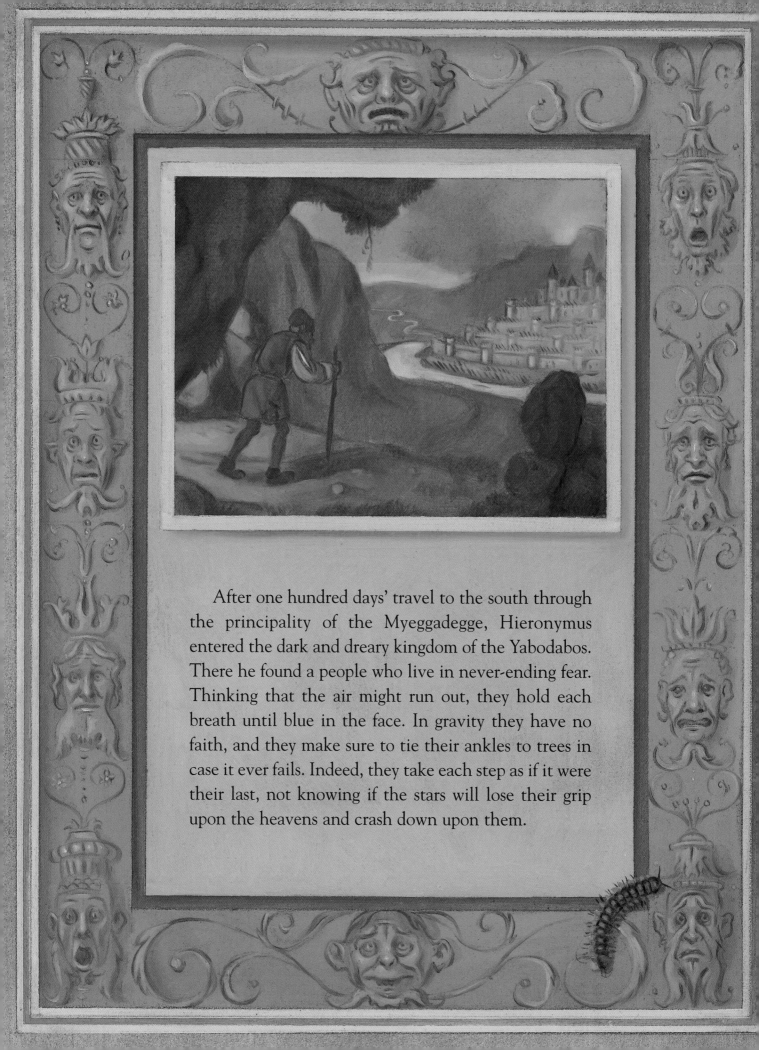

After one hundred days' travel to the south through the principality of the Myeggadegge, Hieronymus entered the dark and dreary kingdom of the Yabodabos. There he found a people who live in never-ending fear. Thinking that the air might run out, they hold each breath until blue in the face. In gravity they have no faith, and they make sure to tie their ankles to trees in case it ever fails. Indeed, they take each step as if it were their last, not knowing if the stars will lose their grip upon the heavens and crash down upon them.

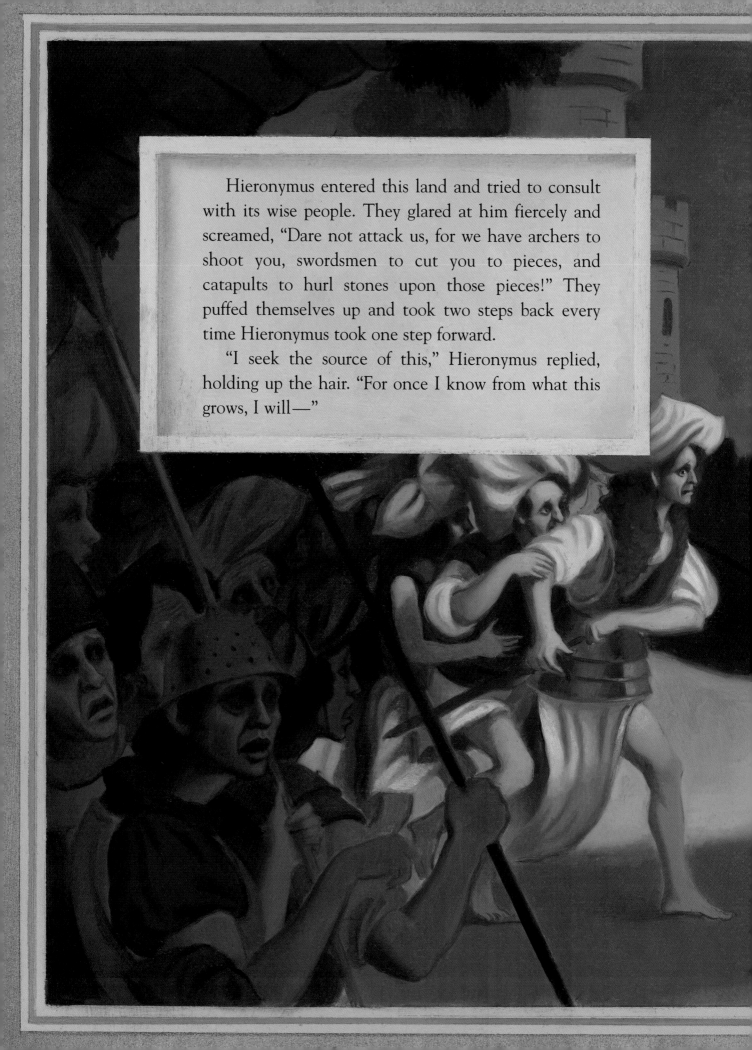

Hieronymus entered this land and tried to consult with its wise people. They glared at him fiercely and screamed, "Dare not attack us, for we have archers to shoot you, swordsmen to cut you to pieces, and catapults to hurl stones upon those pieces!" They puffed themselves up and took two steps back every time Hieronymus took one step forward.

"I seek the source of this," Hieronymus replied, holding up the hair. "For once I know from what this grows, I will—"

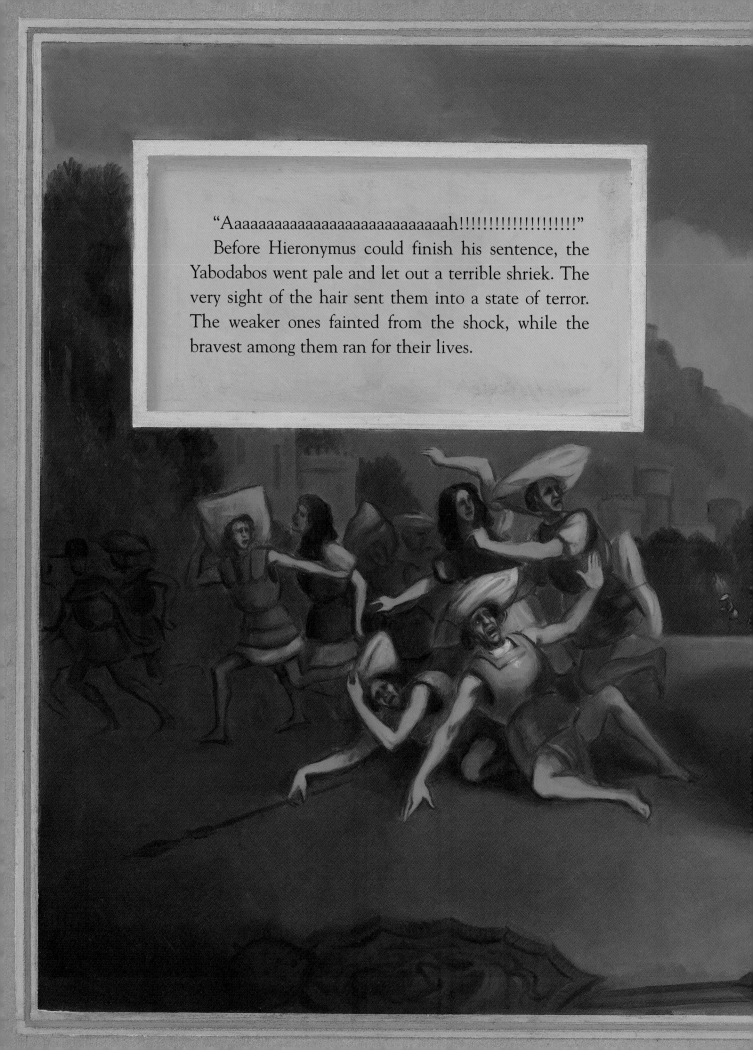

"Aaaaaaaaaaaaaaaaaaaaaaaaaaaaah!!!!!!!!!!!!!!!!!!!!"
Before Hieronymus could finish his sentence, the Yabodabos went pale and let out a terrible shriek. The very sight of the hair sent them into a state of terror. The weaker ones fainted from the shock, while the bravest among them ran for their lives.

Hieronymus kept chasing after the breeze through all four corners of the globe, until one day he looked up and saw that the trail led back to his laboratory. There was nowhere else to search. The chase was over.

Then a storm bore down upon Hieronymus's mind. He tore at his clothes and clawed at the ground in black despair. "I am cursed!" Hieronymus screamed. "Cursed by day and cursed by night! Now I shall never know all that there is to know because of a single little hair!"

Once again, all of the screaming awoke Pieter, who was practicing a new napping maneuver. He turned over and looked at his long-absent master and the mysterious hair through eyes half closed with sleep. "Master," Pieter said, "doesn't that hair come from the top of your head?"

Hieronymus plucked a hair from the top of his head and held it up before his face. And when he saw that what Pieter had said was true, he cried out in disbelief, "For all my knowledge of things great and small, how truly little do I know myself!"

Then Hieronymus sat down and wrote his greatest work, *The Hairiad*, in which—but you know all about it. It was a shining star among books, so great that only one other book eclipsed it: Pieter's ten-volume work, *The Principles of Napology*, written entirely while napping.

So now you're a great knower of things as well. You know about Hieronymus, king of the knowers. You know about the saltiness of ink and the bounciness of sausage. You even know about the squishiness of things. What else do you need to know? That, my dear reader, is not for me to tell you, but for you to find out.